Br

The Barrington Bear

Written by Mark Blackburn &
Illustrated by Alice Jowitt

Hardcover ISBN: 978-1-8380976-0-8

Paperback ISBN: 978-1-8380976-2-2

ebook ISBN: 978-1-8380976-1-5

CONTENTS

Chapter 1:
The Party 7

Chapter 2:
Alone in the Woods 13

Chapter 3:
A Dog's Dinner?. 17

Chapter 4:
A White Christmas 21

Chapter 1

The Party

Lots of people have heard of the Barrington Bear, but not many of them know he's called Brian. He's called Brian because he's a little brown bear and when Mia, the girl who owns him, was younger she thought he was Brian Bear, not a brown bear. So then the whole family called him Brian. He's about the size of your average cat, with a little black button nose and golden eyes.

These days Brian lives happily with Mia and her brother Billy and their mum and dad, but there was a very bad time earlier in Brian's life and everyone knows about it – the terrible tale of the Barrington Bear.

❖ ❖ ❖

Brian still remembers the awful day when everything began to go wrong. It had all started so well. It was a beautiful sunny Autumn afternoon, and the whole family had gone to a garden party in the Big House. That wasn't really its name, but that's what everyone in the village called it, including Mia's parents. Mr and Mrs Binks lived there. Mrs Binks was nice, but Mr Binks was a bit strange – he always wore a top hat, even on a hot day, and he had a very funny walk. People said he had one leg longer than the other.

All the children in the village were welcome. The family were all getting ready in the kitchen before they set off. They were very lucky because the garden of the big house backed onto their own, so they could just walk through a gap in the hedge and then they'd be there, just like that.

"Mum, can I take Brian with us to the party?" Mia asked. She already had his paw glued to her hand.

"Are you sure that's a good idea, darling?" Mum said. "There'll be lots of people there, and he might get lost."

"Oh please, Mum! He won't, I'll hold on to him tight, I won't let him go."

"But what about when you want to eat something? You're bound to want some cake."

"I don't need two hands to eat my cake!"

Mia wore her mum down, and Brian was allowed to come. He was pleased, because he quite liked cake. In fact, he liked it a lot.

Finally they were all ready to go to the party, and they set off down the garden. Although they could get through the hedge, it was still a bit scary, because the Big House had a Big Garden too, and to start with it was all woody and tangly.

There was a path through, but it was overgrown because only the badgers used it. It was quite dark too, as all the trees and leaves grew over the top. It was like going through a haunted tunnel, Brian thought.

There seemed to be lots of noises coming from places Brian couldn't see; he thought it was probably other animals, and he hoped they weren't bigger than him. Unfortunately, most animals were.

As usual, Billy was running on ahead; well, running as fast as he could without tripping over, and he shouted out: "I'm in the Big Garden!" Dad shooshed him, but then they all burst through into bright sunshine and green grass.

Mia and Brian weren't disappointed – there was chocolate cake, and jam tarts, and ice cream. There were even fizzy drinks, which they weren't allowed at home. The grown-ups didn't seem to mind today though – they had their own fizzy drinks and lots of beer, and were laughing and chatting away and not taking much notice.

There were plenty of other children too and when they'd had enough cake, they all started playing hide and seek, running around the Big Garden. As the game went on, the boys and girls were hiding deeper and deeper in the spooky wood between the gardens, so they couldn't be found.

Up to now, Mia had kept her word, and held Brian tight, even when she was eating cake – she'd used just one hand, as she'd promised. And to start with then they played, she'd clutched his little paw. But it was hard running through the wood and holding him, and when she saw a big old tree with a hole under it, she thought she'd hide him in there and come back for him after the game.

From his hole in the tree, Brian could hear the children running around in the wood, and sometimes they ran quite close to him, though no one saw him. He didn't like it down there though; it was dark and damp. He hoped the game would soon be over, and that Mia would come and pick him up and take him home.

Because Mia lived next door, she knew the wood better than most of the other children and she picked a perfect hiding place in the middle of a bush almost back in her own garden. It was like a secret cave – even when the other kids walked straight past the bush they couldn't see her inside.

The garden party came to an end, and still no one had found Mia. All the other children were back with their parents. Her mum and dad started calling – "Mia, where ARE you? You can come out now, you've won."

So Mia came back into the Big Garden, and as she popped through, all the adults clapped and she was given a leftover cake to take home as her prize. For a moment she was thrilled and happy, and then she remembered Brian!

"I've got to go back into the wood", she cried, "I left Brian in there!"

"That's OK", her dad said, "we can all look on the way home."

Mia was sure she would recognise the tree where she'd left Brian, but now they all looked the same. It was starting to get a bit dark too. She would have stayed out all night, but eventually Mum said they had to go home. Mia cried, but Dad promised they'd all come back into the wood the next day and find him.

Brian could hear Mia crying – she was only a few trees away. But as all children know, while little bears can hear you, they can't talk back. So poor Brian couldn't call out and tell her where he was. He just had to listen to her crying, and then the footsteps fading through the wood as the family went home without him. And then nothing.

Chapter 2

Alone in the Woods

Now it was properly getting dark and Brian was hungry, frightened and cold. What was he going to do? Then he heard grunts and footsteps coming closer and closer. Now he was really scared.

He saw their eyes before he saw the rest of them - three pairs glinting in the darkness. He kept still and held his breath but they seemed to know just where he was anyway. Then there they were, right by his tree - three badgers. One was a small one, about his size, and the other two much bigger.

But then one of the bigger ones started to talk - Brian was surprised badgers could talk because he thought only humans could. She had a kind gentle voice.

"What's a little bear doing out here in the wood all on his own at night?"

To his amazement, Brian found that while he couldn't talk to Mia, he could talk to the badgers, and the words came tumbling out... "Mia left me under the tree, then they couldn't find me, and I'm cold, and hungry... They said they'd come back tomorrow, but what will I do?"

"Don't worry little bear, we'll look after you till then."

"I thought badgers were nasty and rough", Brian said.

"Well some of us can be a bit grumpy, but mostly we're pretty nice, like all animals, if you're nice to us. Even Dennis here can be a bit grumpy sometimes," she said, and nodded at the other big badger, who Brian now noticed was even bigger and had grey whiskers. He just grunted back, grumpily.

"Dennis, go and get some food for this poor little bear", she said, and Dennis shuffled off, grumpily.

"So what IS your name, little bear?"

"Brian", said Brian.

"Well Brian, I'm Flo, and this is my daughter Dilly", she said, pointing down at the badger Brian's size, who was half hiding behind her mother. "Say hello, Dilly".

"Hello Brian", said Dilly.

"Hello Dilly", said Brian, and they both looked at each other shyly. At that moment Dennis came back with the some food – nuts and acorns mostly. Brian didn't think he'd like them, but they were actually quite tasty. Especially when you're a hungry little bear.

After supper Flo, the mummy badger, made sure Brian was cosy with a little blanket she'd found in the wood, and they all said good night, the badgers promising him they'd keep an eye on him, and he didn't have to worry.

But still Brian did worry – it was the first time he'd slept out in the open and he was quite scared. He kept hearing noises and thinking he saw things in the shadows and he didn't sleep very much. He was very glad when it started to get light again. Brian didn't know that life was about to get a lot more difficult.

Chapter 3

A Dog's Dinner?

Before the badgers came back the next morning, and before Mia and the family search party could arrive, Mr and Mrs Binks from the Big House were taking their dog Lewis around the edge of the Big Garden. Lewis was a bit bigger than Brian, and had scruffy white fur, and a big mouth for a small dog. When he was near the tree Brian was hidden in, he got a sniff of Brian and his little black nose twitched. Suddenly, before they could stop him, Lewis dashed off into the wood.

Within seconds he found Brian, and picked him up between his jaws – quite gently. Lewis would either eat little bears straight away, or bury them for later, or decide they were his friend. Luckily, he decided Brian would be his friend. He carried him proudly out of the wood back to Mr and Mrs Binks.

“Oh Lewis, where on Earth did you find that?” said Mrs Binks, but they allowed him to carry Brian home, where at least he was cosy.

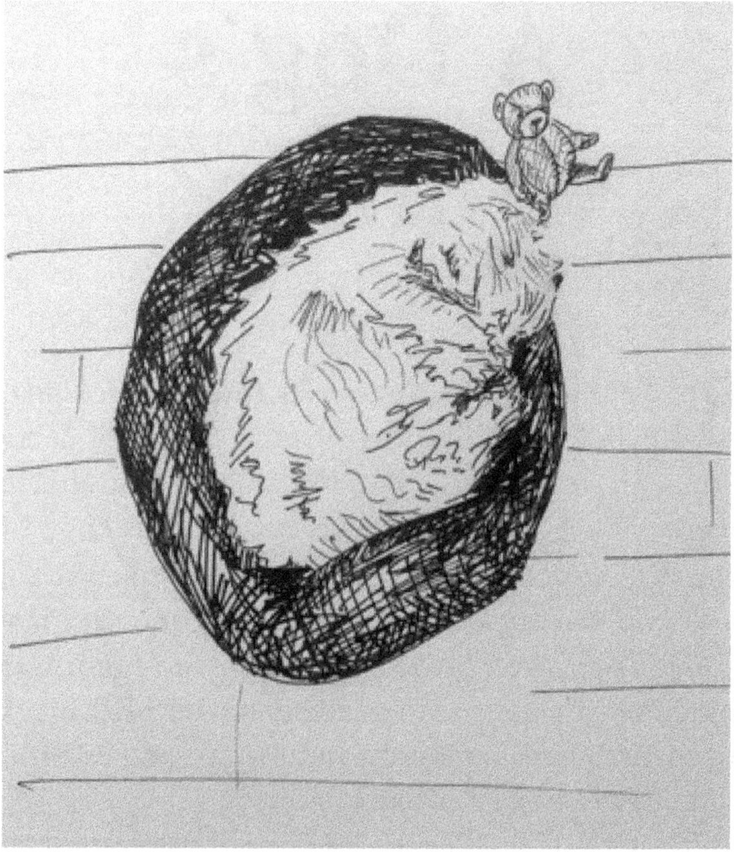

Not much later, Mia and Billy and Mum and Dad were looking all over the woods for Brian, but of course they couldn’t find him. They stopped for lunch and tried again in the afternoon. Only when it got dark did they stop, and Mia cried herself to sleep that night thinking Brian was all alone in the woods.

The next day she had to go to school, but she looked again when she got home, and she did every afternoon until the days got shorter and it was too dark.

The next few weeks passed sadly but quietly; Mia in one house, Brian in another. Brian spent most of his time in Lewis's toy basket, but he was one of Lewis's favourites and he often got him out to play. Still, Brian missed Mia and wondered if he'd ever see her again.

MISSING
have you seen this bear?

Chapter 4

A White Christmas

One day just before Christmas, it was a lovely cold clear sunny day and Mr & Mrs Binks decided they'd walk over the hill with Lewis to the next village, Shepton, to fetch the newspaper. Lewis decided Brian might like the journey, so he brought him, gently carrying him by the scruff of the neck.

On the way back, they were just crossing over the top of the hill when a rabbit ran out right in front of them. Lewis chased straight after him, and dropped Brian, being much more interested in the rabbit.

Of course Lewis didn't catch the rabbit, he never did, but by the time he lost him, Mr and Mrs Binks were at the bottom of the hill, and Lewis ran off after them, forgetting all about Brian.

Mr and Mrs Binks only noticed Brian wasn't there when they got home, but Mr Binks just lifted his top hat, scratched his head and said, "Oh well, someone else's turn to find him now."

Poor old Brian. Now he was outdoors alone again, but this time it was much colder, there wasn't a tree to hide in and there were no badgers to look after him. It got dark very early, and just when Brian thought things couldn't get any worse, it began to... snow.

That night was the worst night of Brian's life. The snow kept falling, and soon it was so deep around him that only his face and the top of his little head were poking out. The darkness seemed to last forever, and he was absolutely frozen by the time it slowly started to get light again.

Then when it got light, a crow flew down thinking his nose was a little berry in the snow. She had a peck and then flew off again in disgust, spitting a piece of his nose out! Poor Brian, freezing cold and now battered and bruised.

Back at Mia's house, it didn't look like being a very happy Christmas either. Whenever her mum asked her what she wanted for her present, Mia just said she wanted Brian back, but there wasn't much anyone could do about that.

Still, when they all woke up on Christmas Eve, it had snowed the night before, and even Mia cheered up a bit as they all went outside to build a snowman. Then Mum and Dad said it was time to walk over to the Carols in Shepton, so they all put on their cosiest coats and their thickest socks and their boots for the march over the hill.

Just when they reached the very top, the strangest thing happened. Mia had started to get miserable again, and she was dawdling behind, but then she thought she heard her name being called by a tiny, faint voice.

Brian had been lying in the snow all morning, and although the sun had come out again, it was still very cold and the snow wasn't melting much. He wondered if he'd ever escape or if he'd just be stuck there forever. For the first time he'd ever known, a little tear ran down his cheek, but then is stopped half way, and froze.

Just at the moment when he thought he was the saddest a little bear could be, he heard voices coming up the hill. Then he realised they weren't just voices – it was Mia and her family!

But they were getting closer and closer and they hadn't seen him. No wonder, only part of his little head was sticking out of the snow! First Dad walked past, within a few feet of him, then Billy, then Mum! Now only Mia was still to pass! He had to do something!

He remembered he'd been able to talk to the badgers, so now he tried really, really hard... "Mia! Mia!"

He could do it! He could do it! She heard that faint cry, looked down towards him, and a moment later she bent down, pulled him out of the snow, and started brushing it off him and smothering him with kisses. "Mum, Dad, I've found Brian!" she half-cried, half-shouted.

Of course, no one believed she'd heard him call her name, but Brian and Mia didn't care – they were just pleased to be together again. And everyone wondered how Brian had come to be buried in the snow with a piece of his nose missing at the top of the hill between Barrington and Shepton, but they didn't really care either, because Mia was happy again.

Of course when Mia woke up on Christmas morning, she did have other presents, but the best present of all was Brian being there too – a bit older, a bit scruffier, but still the same old Brian. As for Brian, he decided he was never going outside again. Ever.

From that day on, he never spoke to humans again either. But then he didn't need to.

The End

Lightning Source UK Ltd.
Milton Keynes UK
UKHW021830180921
390798UK00011B/106

9 781838 097622